The Visits of the (

By the same author

C. G. Jung and Hermann Hesse. A Record of Two Friendships

The Ultimate Flower

The Visits of the Queen of Sheba

Miguel Serrano

Foreword by

C. G. Jung

Illustrated by
Julio Escamez

Translated by
Frank MacShane

Routledge & Kegan Paul
London and Boston

First published 1960
by P. S. Jayasinghe,
Asia Publishing House,
Bombay
Second edition 1972
by Routledge & Kegan Paul Ltd
Broadway House, 68–74 Carter Lane,
London EC4V 5EL
Printed in Great Britain by
W & J Mackay Limited, Chatham

ISBN 0 7100 7341 0 (c)
ISBN 0 7100 7399 2 (p)

In former years we used to think that you and I were one. How does it happen, then, that now you are yourself and I am myself?

Bhartrihari

Sometimes in the ocean a piece of wood bumps into another only to float away again. So it is with human beings.

Mahabharata

Foreword

This book is an extraordinary piece of work. It is dreams within dreams, highly poetic I should say and most unlike the spontaneous products of the unconscious I am used to, although well-known archetypic figures are clearly discernible. The poetic genius has transformed the primordial material into almost musical shapes, as, on the other side, Schopenhauer understands Music as the movement of archetypic ideas. The chief moulding and shaping factor seems to be a strong aesthetical tendency. Consequently the effect on the reader captivates him in an increasing dream, in an ever extending space and an immeasurable depth of time. On the other hand the cognitive element plays no significant role, it even recedes into a misty background yet alive with the wealth of colourful images. The unconscious, or whatever we designate by this name, presents itself to the author by its poetic aspect, which I envisage chiefly from its scientific and philosophic—or perhaps more accurate—from its religious aspect. The Unconscious is surely the *Pammeter*, the Mother of All (i.e. of all psychical life), being the matrix, the background and foundation of all the differentiated phenomena we call psychical: religion, science, philosophy and art. Its experience—in whatever form it may be—is an approach to wholeness, the one experience absent in our modern civilization. It is the avenue and via regia to the Unus Mundus.

C. G. Jung.

Küsnacht-Zürich,
14 January 1960.

Contents

Plates

The Great Mother

In the beginning, the Great Mother looked at herself in a mirror. Then she looked at a second mirror and at a third. In this way all mothers came into being. The Great Mother had eyes like the depths of an abyss, but those of the other mothers were as blue as the sky.

In the ancient city of Amber, next to the Temple of Kali, a priest wearing a red tunic and with feet covered with the blood of sacrifices, explained these things to me. And so I came to know that I had not one mother but many.

Since my life seems to have been so much like an abyss and to be more and more like one, I am trying to look within myself to discover the coffin of the original Great Mother. I will open it and inside I will probably find that she has taken the form of somebody else. Perhaps she will be the Queen of Sheba; possibly even Jesus Christ. Whatever form she takes will be the form of my soul.

Of course when one opens a coffin, one destroys it. Nevertheless a delicate odour of cedarwood will come forth.

The River

Once I went to Mount Kailas where the great god, Siva, lives. I watched him dance and he taught me how to dance and forget. As a result, I dance one day in the sun and another in the shade. Since going to Mount Kailas I have become like a river which cannot be held back.

I then came down from the sacred mountain which is high in the Himalayas beyond the rain line, and went down to Cape Comorin where the waters of three ancient seas are joined together.

And I saw that there were temples in both places.

1 I came to know that I had not one mother but many . . .

The Story of the Moonstone

The ring you see on my finger is a moonstone. When the third moon fell onto the earth, it fell into the sea. Sinking into the waters, it sent up bubbles, like the last breath of a drowning man. These bubbles became moonstones.

Centuries later, when the glacial ices retreated towards the poles, leaving Aryana Vaiji abandoned and the sunny city of Avalon turned into a city of death, the first human beings, men with blue eyes and blond hair, risked their lives in the water to gather moonstones. They set them in their stone daggers and placed them on their foreheads so that they might be able to see the ancient City of Dawn, called Aryana Vaiji and the former City of the Sun, called Avalon. In this way, the moonstone became the third eye, showing men what their blue eyes could not see.

The men of those early times were called Walkers of the Dawn, and their women, whose hair was also blond and whose eyes were deep blue like the waters where the moonstone was found, were called Guardians of the Dawn. These women placed the moonstone between their breasts.

In time, the men went to their women for the moonstone, so that they might contemplate the City of Dawn and the City of the Sun. If they did not perish in the wild torrents of water, they were lost between the white breasts of their women.

This is the story of eternal love, which is born among the ices but which is soon mixed with dreams of death and of a new dawn. The first heroes were those who surrendered themselves to the holocaust of love. As they died, they caught a last glimpse of the City of Dawn and felt for the last time the milky lightning of the moon.

The first conquerors of the earth, on the other hand, were those who refused love and instead chose as their symbol the white fleece of the ram. Following a messiah, they marched over the earth and made it their own. What they were looking for was an Avalon of this world. For them the moonstone had a different meaning. They merely put it between their eyes in the same way they held their daggers in their hands. Their messiah, whose name changes with the ages, was to them merely the first Walker of the Dawn. Their real emblem was the ram's fleece.

When I first looked at the moonstone, I was told by a wise man what it signified. 'It points two ways', he said. 'One really leads to perdition although it pretends to do otherwise, while the other leads you to an empty oasis where men stand alone on the ices holding their battle swords. In order to survive you must be brave; you must seize the stone dagger and kill eternal love.'

For many years I followed his advice and tried to stifle the love that is in me. I wandered far and wide over the earth. I would watch the morning star and I would think I had discovered the City of Dawn. In the end I became a pilgrim. My skin became dry and my hair grew down to my shoulders. I joined an ancient tribe of wanderers and walked with them across the earth. They all carried stone daggers and worshipped the moonstone.

First we wandered towards the Antarctic ices which are near my own homeland and there we met an ancient prophet who guided us. He seemed to be a reincarnation of some ancient holy man. We also had a dog with us who helped guide us towards the primeval oasis.

At the crucial moment I weakened, however; the howling of the winds and the wailing of the dog had brought to mind the calm voice of eternal love, and I fled from the place. For a short while I tried to find peace by the edge of the sea, but in the end I rejoined my former comrades. Together we continued to traverse the earth; we fought battles, captured cities and visited ancient temples where pagan rites are still practised. I tried to give up everything, I took up the burden of the cross and even tried to make it rotate like the holy swastika. There was nothing I did not do to try to kill the love within me and to try to find the ancient city which existed before love began.

Finally I came to India, and there I began to worship Siva. I tried to subdue my will to his: I prostrated myself before his altar and remained perfectly still for years in an effort to recover the lost vision of the City of Dawn. Although my body remained still, my mind would wander across the southern ices and I was once again with the warrior-pilgrims with their stone daggers. Others would also be with me: some were beggars, others kings. But everybody in the ancient India of Siva knew that only by abandoning their bodies could they attain the ancient City of Dawn. That is why there are so many abandoned bodies along the roads of India, and that is why, in India, the heat of the sun burns the ram's fleece.

Often I remembered the dog that had given up its soul to guide us through the icy wastes of the south. I was reminded of it by the howling of the many dogs in India. But now its howl seemed different, as though it were mourning its lost fleece, and as if it had stopped being a symbol and had begun to feel and therefore to weep.

Then one day, while I was kneeling beside the bed of a dying girl to whom I was telling the story of the moonstone, love suddenly came again, overthrowing all my asceticism and turning me onto the other path suggested by the stone in my ring. I felt I was robbed of all I had gained. My body was returned to me, but my soul was destroyed. By that time, however, my body had half withered away because of the many years I had spent by the sacred mountain of the Lord Siva. I went down to the holy lake called Manasarovar, which adjoins Mount Kailas. There I washed with care and, moving out towards the centre of the lake, submerged my body and sank it to the depths of the sacred waters. As the body drowned, it sent forth its last breath exactly like the breath of the moonstone. After a bit, it rose again to the surface, but it was now combined with the body of the dog that had died years before in the Antarctic ices. My new body had the head of that golden-haired dog.

Now I no longer hear the anguished howl of that dog, wailing for its lost body.

I have given up the teachings of the wise man, and I have exchanged the stone dagger for the flute. Now I sing the old songs of the sun and dance to music. The ring I have long since thrown into the sea because now I look for the City of Dawn amongst the breasts of beautiful women. I am ready now for the altar of the goddess Kali.

I am dying, but as I expire like a hero who no longer looks for Avalon in the distance, I find that, without my wanting it and without my hoping for it, a moonstone begins to appear between my eyebrows.

Parvati

One day as she passed along the road outside my house she smiled at me. Her teeth were even and white, but her smile was hesitant, like the reflection of sugar-cane in a river gently stirred by the wind.

Then on an afternoon some days later she came to my study where I keep a stone statue of Siva. This statue shows Siva with his eyes closed as though he were dreaming. He observes only what passes in the interior of his mind: he appears to be listening, as to the sound of approaching steps that may lead to the top of the Tree of Paradise or even to within sight of the City of Dawn. The statue also portrays Siva's ambiguous smile: *there is one smile for love, another for hatred and a third for both.* Siva always smiles in this manner. His smile is a mixture of pleasure, misery, and ecstasy.

And there, at the foot of the statue, stood the beautiful girl called Parvati—who also smiled. She was tall and strong. Her hair and skin were dark and she looked like a woman from Bengal and also as though she had come from that ancient region that had once been touched by Atlantis and which had rested quietly under the Flood. For that is the real India: there the deserts begin and there the cobra forests, the mountains of Assam, the sea of Orissa and the living stream of Brahmaputra all meet. Standing by the statue, Parvati then began to remove her sari, and as she did so, she revealed a body that seemed to come from another world. And the aroma that came from her was like a mixture of sugar-cane and sweet wine, of jasmin and dreams, of the sky and the river: it was something like fine rich tea or sandalwood.

I quickly went up to her to kiss her open mouth. At first she received my kiss like a nervous child. But when I began to caress her, she became agitated like the islands of Atlantis rising from the sea and revealing buried cities, forests and fields. As her perfume encompassed me, I found my old world buried in this new flood and, amongst strange words from remote epochs, amongst sighs echoing forth from dead civilizations, I moved my hand towards the moonstone that hung between her breasts—on that ancient sacrificial altar—so that I might have a glimpse of the City of Dawn. And as I died there I turned to the statue of Siva to thank him for the gift of this woman. 'Thank you,' I cried, 'for having given me this marvellous creature. Thank you for this gift wrapped in sandalwood and blue sky—this gift that represents all India. Thank you for this extreme good fortune.'

Stretched out side by side, we looked at and caressed each other, speaking without words. Little by little her eyes became soft and gentle like those of a virgin or those of Kanyakumari, the virgin princess of Cape Comorin which lies at the extreme end of India where the waters of three great seas meet. The aspect of Kali, the devouress, had disappeared and become only a dream locked up in the dismal depths of the subconscious.

Then she rose, and when I asked her who she was she told me her name was Parvati. At that moment the head of the statue looked as though it wanted to move so that Siva could observe what was happening and come out of his dream. Of course this girl also knew that Parvati is Siva's wife. I then pointed out the statue of the god and said: 'See how he smiles at you. He really is your husband.'

'No,' she then said, 'you are.'

And at that moment I was ready to believe it.

Then she went away. My wife from Atlantis, my Indian wife, my wife for that day—for she was all in one—walked slowly like a queen, which is how all the true women of India walk, away from me. I shall never see her again in this life, for I don't really know who she was or where she came from. One day she walked along the road outside of my house and passed an evening with me. I gave her part of my life so that I might touch the moonstone and see the City of Origins. And that is all there is.

I had fallen asleep beneath the statue of Siva and I dreamed that he spoke to me and told me that in Bengal where the hills are full of snakes, he was called An and his wife, Uma. 'It's simply a question of names,' he explained. 'I have so many names I can easily give you Parvati, keeping Uma for myself. And you can be Siva if you want because I can always remain An.' He then spoke to me about the Brahmaputra. 'That river can teach you everything,' he said. 'Day after day the water goes by. What you see today is lost and gone tomorrow. Yet, although the water disappears, the river remains: therefore its source is eternal. It is renewed in the deep springs of the earth and from the snows melting in the high mountains. There is a central force in the world that is never spent or exhausted. It is found in many places—as much in the high mountains and the oasis of the ices as in the breasts of Parvati or Uma. Even though you die a thousand times, if you die loving truth you will be like the Brahmaputra and you will always come back. Therefore it is important to be calm like the waters of the river and not to be possessive. Parvati has gone away, but it doesn't matter that the wife of one day is lost, for other days will bring other Parvatis. *The sun also ariseth, and the sun goeth down, and hasteth to the place where he arose. . . . All the rivers run into the sea; yet the sea is not full; unto the place from whence the rivers came, thither they return again.*'

I awoke with my face turned towards the stone statue. Watching it, I found I was told many more things. *The sea was in your veins*, it said. As I looked at the smiling face of the statue, I realized its smile was like Parvati's at the moment of pleasure. It was a smile of love as much as of hate, of divine ecstasy and of death, of carnal and sacred love. And so Parvati had laughed and cried in my arms, prayed and cursed, loved me and despised me—all these in the space of a few moments. But then she had had the same wise and true expression of the stone statue, for *the sea was in her veins* as well.

Then, without taking my eyes from Siva, I began to murmur an answer to his teaching.

'No,' I said, 'I am no river and no sea runs in my veins. I am not ready for that. I need to dream more, to be caught again in your net and to burn my wings. Let me have her once again. Make her walk again along the path outside my house. I want to be overcome by her perfume, I must drown myself in her eyes, lie on her sacrificial altar and die as I again behold the moonstone. . . .'

Siva neither moved nor spoke. Only the mournful smile remained.

Then it fell like a drop of water slipping through the night. Trembling, I knew what it meant. 'You will have her again and shall find her—but only within yourself, and not from without.'

Sadly I bowed my head.

2 I have become like a river which cannot be held back

The Visits of the Queen of Sheba

Set me as a seal upon thine heart,
As a seal upon thine arm:
For love is strong as death.

My belief in reincarnation first brought me to India. Since I have no proof of it, I cannot be sure of this belief, but I accept it as true and carry on in a dreamlike fashion. So it goes for days and months, and then suddenly the Queen of Sheba appears to me, and I know that my belief is true. For when she comes I have a feeling of certainty and know that my values are right. Usually I don't realize this truth until after she has left—which is probably natural since only in absence do we recognize and yearn for each other. Only after she has gone do I know that my vague notion about reincarnation is true, and that my soul is as old, or almost as old, as hers is.

The concept of reincarnation is curiously ironical, when you think about it. You would imagine that two persons who had been intimate for five thousand years would recognize each other immediately when they meet—yet they don't. At first there is always a little tension, almost a kind of hostility between thc two. This surely is peculiar when you consider how much there is in common between them—or between us, for I am speaking of the Queen of Sheba and myself. We have had so many nights of love, we share so many happy memories, and also so many sad ones, you would think we would recognize each other immediately. Yet at first she always seems so distant I am almost irritated. Afterwards I think it is strange that I did not throw myself at her feet and weep for joy, that I did not grasp her hands and gaze into her eyes.

Yet I never do. It's as though I'm always only half awake when we meet to exchange gifts. To be sure, the mist rises a little when we repeat the splendid pattern of our love. And I say to her: *Thy two breasts are like two young roes that are twins, which feed among the lilies. Thy lips, O my spouse, drop as the honey-comb: honey and milk are under thy tongue; and the smell of thy garments is like the smell of Lebanon. . . .* My speech may be music, but to me it is only a distant echo reverberating in my memory.

Five thousand years ago, the Queen of Sheba lived in Sumeria, alongside the sunny valley of the Euphrates. When she died, her head was sheathed with gold leaf, and she was buried in Ur. You would think that I would recognize her when she comes, but my memory is so bad that only her eyes seem familiar.

Over the millenniums it is possible that the colour of her eyes may have changed but their quiet expression never does. They always appear to be faintly puzzled at the idea that her body should turn to dust when she still had so many thousands of years to live.

One day some archaeologists found her head in Ur, and they placed it in a museum. After her last visit, I had a photograph taken of this head so that I would not forget it. Yet even that was naïve, since it would only be helpful if the Queen of Sheba were to visit me in this life and during my present incarnation. But the Queen of Sheba has already come and gone.

Greater grief hath no man. . . .

Who is this that cometh out of the wilderness
Like a pillar of smoke,
Perfumed with myrrh and frankincense,
With all powders of the merchant?

As it happened, I was praying when the Queen came. I was trying to concentrate on the syllable OM which means the beginning and the end and which is the note upon which the Lord Brahma created the world. The syllable must be pronounced with a concentration of all the body and soul. If the meditation is properly performed, the body begins to feel a soft smarting sensation, and the fingertips begin to tingle. Having reached this stage, I seemed to hear the distant chanting of a Hindu family carrying a dead relative down to the sacred river Jumna. On the bank of the river, the pyre of sandalwood would be waiting. Then it would be set on fire while round about the relatives would sing to Rama and to the shepherd, Krishna, the colour of whose skin was blue. There was no unhappiness: merely a grain returning to the field, a drop of water rejoining the eternal stream. O Bhagawan, Bhagawan. . . .

Then suddenly she entered and sat down next to me. I was surprised, for she was interrupting my prayer. I tried to turn my face away and to go on with the syllable OM, but something made me look at her. She was not obviously beautiful, but her eyes were luminous and at the same time dark, like a patch of shadow surrounded by bright sunlight. Paradoxically, this shadow, which after all represents the darkness of tombs and decay and age, made her appear young. Yet I could not concentrate on her face because of the sharp contrasts between shadow and light. Instead, I looked at her hands. It was strange that fingers which had been buried for centuries under the desert sands should shed such beauty and passion.

Then softly she began to sing:

Return little flower of dust,
Rise at the sound of the flute
And dance with the golden-horned god.
Spring comes again to our island,
The grapes are prepared for the bull.
When the harvest comes, remember
The flute of the child god, our Lord.

While she sang I recalled the old priestesses of Crete who, in the blue Mediterranean, worshipped the sacred minotaur. Then suddenly I became happy and forgot about the syllable OM. I felt the music of a flute within myself. It was a flute played by those same fingers that had long laid buried under the desert sands, the same fingers as those of the blue god which were given vitality by the golden grapes—as they were long ago in the springtime of Ur.

Then quietly I spoke:

'Are you by chance,' I asked, 'a pilgrim in search of the fountains of life? For if you are, you should go to the dreamy city of Banaras where a clue to the secret may be found. Otherwise travel to Mount Kailas, the dwelling place of the Lord Siva at the roof of the world, at the top of the Tree of Life. . . .'

But she remained silent, looking at me from her shadowed brilliance. Then she moved nearer, holding out for me her first gift—a golden cape, like the ceremonial dress of some ancient Maharajah of Udaipur.

'This,' she said, 'belongs to you.'

And when I touched it, running my fingers over the rich gold embroidery, I recognized it. It really was mine.

I stood up and walked into the large hall where I keep my sacred paintings. For a long time I stared at a Tibetan 'tanka' which represented the Tree of Life. At the top, amongst the leaves, Padmasambhava is shown embracing his goddess. They were united as one. On the top of the Tree of Life—in the Hall of the Palace—someone had found somebody for whom he had been searching for a long, long time. And the tears of joy which were shed became the fruit of the Tree of Life, the grapes whose juice is distilled by the flute of the blue god.

I then picked up a cane which resembled a shepherd's staff, and also looked like a snake. It was embossed with silver and its handle was carved in the shape of a lion's head with emeralds for eyes. In the centre, a small ruby marked the position of the third eye, the one that is capable of seeing the Hall of the Palace on the Tree of Life and which understands the symbolism of that love scene.

I went out and gave it to her, saying: 'This is yours; it has always been yours. Don't you recognize it? It too comes from Udaipur. Once I think it belonged to Queen Padmani, who preferred to die by burning than to be unfaithful. It is called "Kundalini" because it looks like a snake.'

She took it and began to fondle it. It was as though she were touching the flute of the blue god, the flute of Siva which is the 'lingam' of the Sun. She closed her eyes to feel and enjoy it better and as she did this, I was able for the first time to see her face. With its light extinguished, the shape of the planet was visible. Her forehead wide and pale as the moon, was that of my beloved Queen. It was sheathed with gold and her hair was damp with frankincense and myrrh.

Then I wanted to throw myself at her feet and worship her. But I couldn't, because I still did not wholly recognize her and because it was almost . . . it was almost. . . .

I am my beloved's
And my beloved is mine;
She feedeth among the lilies.

Across the harbour from Bombay there is an island called Elephanta where a famous cave temple was constructed during the sixth century by the Brahmans. Inside the cave there is a gigantic Trimurti, which is a statue of the god, Siva, in his aspects of god, goddess, and son. It is like Father, Son, and Holy Ghost.

Originally the Trimurti was different. But when the Portuguese came—or perhaps it was the Moslems—the statue was mutilated and its beauty destroyed, or at least altered. There are times when the act of disfigurement increases and completes beauty, for imperfection is the essence of beauty. The Queen of Sheba, for example, is not beautiful in a vulgar, complete way, but her slight imperfections make her beauty special and rare.

At any rate, years ago one of the heads of the great statue at Elephanta was apparently removed. Originally what is now Trimurti was Tetramurti. The mysterious fourth head had been carved on the back, looking backwards upon five thousand years of the past, gazing towards Ur, towards Mohenjodaro, or Harappa, or Aryana Vaija; even towards Avalon, the dead city of Atlantis. This fourth head, in a word, represented the fourth dimension, and its aspect was that of the Son of Death. Here indeed was the true head of the god who is united with his goddess on top of the Tree of Life, and his terrible face expresses the ineffable pleasure of whoever observes the Queen of Sheba playing the flute, the sexual 'lingam' of creation. Yet because it was thought to be indecent, the fourth head was cut off, and now nobody remembers it. I myself had forgotten it until the visit of the Queen of Sheba. Even the old Brahmans had forgotten it. They murmured the verses of a Bhagavad Gita and of an expurgated Ramayana. The Huns of Mihiragula, the invaders from Samarkand, Alfonso de Albuquerque, and all of the East India Company had combined to turn off the light, and the truth of the Tetramurti was expunged from the ancestral Gita and Ramayana.

But the secret still remains in the cave of Elephanta. Next to the Trimurti is a dancing figure of Siva carved from stone. Here is the secret, for the dancing god is bisexual. His right side is that of a man, but his left side is that of a woman. No Eve has yet been fashioned from his rib, but there is a marvellous sculptured breast equal to the Queen of Sheba's, like a 'young roe feeding among the lilies'. In this figure the Queen of Sheba has at long last come again.

The faces of the Trimurti meditate in their three dimensions, and whether they be god the father, god the mother, or god the son, they all hope for the return of the Queen of Sheba. With their closed eyes they dream of her, and they imagine they see her walking across the burning sands of the earth. It is pleasant to look at these stone faces, but it is also sad. In a three-dimensional world, the Queen of Sheba may come, but not to stay.

Greater grief hath no man. . . .

I charge you, O ye daughters of Jerusalem
By the roes, and by the hinds of the field,
That ye stir not up,
Nor wake my love,
Till she please.

On the evening of her visit I was listening to the faraway chants of the Hindus burning a dead relative on the sandalwood pyres by the sacred river Jumna, and I remember that their song mixed with the drumbeat of my heart and the reverberation of the magic syllable OM that ran through my fingertips. Then she approached, and taking me by the hand, led me far away, to the distant beach of Madras. She said that the South of India was a happy place for us because it was farther down, and I knew what she meant.

I wore my golden cape and she leaned on her silver 'Kundalini'. Of course she didn't need a cane because she is young and beautiful, but her five thousand years needed it.

It was during the golden month of May when the heat starts in India. The air was dry and hot, and the earth was beginning to crack. The Bay of Bengal exuded a thick vapour as from a great sea beast, but the sky was full of stars. There were thousands upon thousands of them.

She lay down on the burning sands which have been her bed for so many centuries and looked up at the sky. 'It hasn't changed,' she said. 'It is the same and always will be. How young we are in comparison to the sky!'

I also lay down and rested my head on her lap. Soon the bones of my head began to recognize the bones of her knees—which is not surprising, since there is not a bone of her body unknown to me.

Presently some dark and noisy children arrived and started to dance in the dusk, under the great sky. As they danced, they muttered crude and profane songs. They were completely naked and danced in circles. Then they ran into the sea and came back, dripping foam and perspiring. Once again they began their infernal dance. Would they never leave us in peace? We wanted to be alone after such a long time.

Finally I gave them money, and then they asked for more. Always more. They were the ghosts of India, dark hallucinations forever coming between me and the Queen of Sheba, capable of destroying everything.

They sang in Tamil—or perhaps it was old Sumerian, and they continued to dance: *The mandrakes are loosening their perfume. . . .*

Then in the distance a fisherman appeared, dragging his nets and playing a flute. The boys disappeared as if by magic.

It is like that in India: you must know how to wait.

We stretched out on the sand and I pressed her head against my heart. It is strange, but with her ear I could hear the beating of my own heart. And it was as if the solemn blinking of the stars was keeping time with my heartbeat.

To the rhythm of the planets and of the flute of the Hindu fisherman we softly fell asleep—in that month of May, that summer in Madras.

And that night was another day.

The Visits of the Queen of Sheba

Stay me with flagons,
Comfort me with apples:
For I swoon from love.

We woke up with the water of high tide on our legs. There was no one else on the beach. The fisherman had gone and the stars were obscured by low clouds. I embraced her and she wrapped her body in mine. Softly I breathed in her ear words that echoed the Song of Songs: 'At last you have come,' I said, 'Your thighs are as long as the Indian summer, and they are as hot as the summer's heat, even under the water of the ocean sea. *O Prince's daughter: the joints of thy thighs are like jewels.* Your breasts are the breasts of the Virgin of the Temple at Cape Comorin where the waters of three ancient seas meet. They are the small dry breasts of a virgin queen. Because it is time they were watered by the sea, I will make the waves rise with my lips. And then like doves they will take flight and they will dance like roes through the fields. They will send a message to that shadowy region within you that I have come. Then in that ancient and hidden region, in that ancient Ur, upon that throne of a Sulamite, I will make the sun come out. I will make it shine with my lips and my burning verses which will be as the music of the flute of the blue god. O, how beautiful you are, my Sulamite! *Thy lips, O my spouse, drop as the honey-comb: honey and milk are under thy tongue. You are a fountain of gardens, a well of living waters. . . .*'

Then between our warm kisses she began to sing:

The grapes have returned to our land,
And spring has come to our island,
From the floor of the sea he rises,
The god of the golden horns.
Hail to the singing boy, our Lord.

Then something quite unexpected happened. Whether it was by fate or by chance I do not know. Perhaps they are the same. I was so engrossed in my singing, and in my love, that I gradually penetrated her body. I came to understand it and literally to take possession of it. Apparently the same thing happened to her. I took possession of her soul and she took possession of mine. I was she and she was I. Then

3 Who is this that cometh out of the wilderness?

when the pleasure of love came, when the wave rose over us, I felt with her soul and her body, and she felt with mine. I was at the same time Siva and Parvati, and she was both the Queen of Sheba and Solomon.

That is the mystery of Elephanta.

That is the secret which is now forgotten by the world, which no longer appears in the pages of any Gita or Ramayana. And I discovered it on the burning sands of Madras, beside the Bay of Bengal.

Then she rose and danced naked towards the sea. I followed her, playing the lively flute of the blue god. And together we sang:

Hail, Blue Shepherd of Heaven,
The heart of the Gopis is ripe;
You are purple with passion
Like the grapes of our distant island,
And the throne of the Sulamite of Ur.

And then she disappeared, quietly and suddenly across the sea. And only then was I sure that she had been the Queen of Sheba, my Queen who had come back after such a long time, only to leave me once again.

And I felt as Rama must have felt when the demon with the ten heads and twenty arms stole his beloved Sita from him when they were together in the forest.

Return, return, O Sulamite,
Return, return,
That we may look upon thee.

Ever since the Queen of Sheba went away, I have been sitting alone in my room, thinking. Once again I look at my sacred paintings from Tibet, but when I wear my golden tunic, everything takes on a different meaning. I don't dare repeat the syllable OM because I still hope my Queen may return to rekindle our brief love. It is curious that the heart of a man yearning for eternity should want to obliterate the very pathway he has already cleared.

Sitting alone, I remember my many years of pilgrimage in India. But now everything seems changed. Now I want to be like a river, like the Holy Ganges which rises in the Himalayas, waters the parched land and carries along with it leaves and branches of trees, the bodies of animals and men and even of gods before it reaches the quiet sea. The river does not pick and choose: it welcomes everything. It is neither light nor darkness: it is merely movement towards the sea.

Then I remember that like a river I too have travelled to the Tibetan Himalayas and stood at the foot of the sacred mountain, Kailas, where, beyond the rain line, Lord Siva and the Enlightened Buddha live. Like the river, I too have gone down to the end of India, to Cape Comorin where the three ancient seas meet. And I have seen that there are temples at both extremes.

I learned this truth from the body of the Queen of Sheba, for her body is like the world. And this knowledge was the second gift she gave me.

While the king sitteth at his table,
My spikenard sendeth forth the smell thereof.

One night in November—it was the fifth of the month and thus a day marked by destiny—I was wearing my golden cape from Udaipur and sitting in an old Chinese armchair. The winter had already begun, and it was cold in Old Delhi. After a while I began to feel drowsy and soon I was asleep. Then in a dream I found myself on a road standing by a high tower. Something fell down from above, and a young man who was there handed it to me. It was a small white flower, a diminutive sunflower. 'We all know where it comes from,' said the young man, 'and who sent it to you.' I looked up and realized that she had thrown it so that I would know where she was. I ran towards the tower, found a ladder and hastily climbed to the top. There, in a rectangular space, she stood looking over a balcony. She heard me arrive and throw myself at her feet, and she said to me: 'Now you are mine alone. Before you were one of many, but now I have killed all the others. I suppose that is a crime. . . .'

'Yes,' I answered, 'If it were not a crime, it would not be as it is. . . .'

When I woke up, I found her in my arms, or so it seemed, with her warmth and the light of her eyes. The vision took a long time to vanish, and it seemed more real than reality.

When she had finally gone, this time perhaps forever, I discovered a small white flower lying on the golden crosses of my royal cape.

This was the third gift that she brought me.

Awake, O north wind;
And come, thou south;
Blow upon my garden,
That the spices thereof may flow out.

Outside, the night drums were beating, and the faithful were singing their chants of praise as they walked towards the river where the bodies washed today would be consumed by fire tomorrow. Shapes, smoke-encircled shapes, in the nets of Maya, illusions. . . .

High above, in the blue-grey sky, the Morning Star appeared.

Greater joy hath no man. . . .

The Brother of Silence

He first came some years ago and told me that he wanted to listen to my silence. In the manner of the country he uncovered his feet and sat with crossed legs in a corner of the room. There he remained for a long time until evening came and I could no longer see his face. He had a small dog with him which lay curled up on the hem of his Tibetan monk's robe.

With the coming of dusk, he began to tell me his story. He comes from Almora which is the gateway in the Himavat that leads to Mount Kailas. He likes to stay there and listen to the silence that comes from the Himalayas. He was not born in Almora, however, but much farther to the north by the side of the sea where the moonstone rose from the water. When he was there he used to sit on the beach and listen to the silence of the sea. But people did not understand him there and so he had to leave in search of a place where he would not be molested in his attempt to discover the language of silence.

And so Sunya Bai, the brother of silence, went to Tibet which is the best place in the world for silence. There he usually lives, conducting a silent dialogue with the snow-capped peaks of the Himalayas. Occasionally he comes to Delhi, but only when he thinks it necessary to start a special dialogue in silence with some special person about whom he has been told in the Himavat.

Perhaps that is why he came to see me. At any rate, he asked me not to talk and merely sat down in his Tibetan robe with his dog and listened to my silence. Soon he was conversing with my soul without my knowing it.

Finally he spoke and told me about himself. He said he was not interested in what human beings can say with words; he was only interested in their silence. 'There are people who speak well,' he said, 'but they often have a very bad silence.' He said it was the silence that mattered because it was a preparation for eternal silence.

Then he got up and went to the door. I ran after him and asked him his name. He turned round and said he was called Ernest, and then he went away. It is curious, but it was only then that I realized he was a man and not a woman. For a while I had believed that the strangely robed figure was an ancient woman. In fact, he really had no sex.

For a long time I wondered what we talked about in our silent dialogue. Many years have gone by since that first visit and I still have not found out. From time to time he returns quite unexpectedly and sits in a corner to listen to my silence. The last time he was with me he sat in the same place where the Queen of Sheba had sat, and then I realized that he had been talking about her all the time and that I had been asking him about her return. I looked up and noticed that Ernest was smiling.

Last night he came for the last time. He was alone and remained standing all the time he was with me. In his hand was a pilgrim's staff. He said he was travelling to Sikkim and that although he was seventy years old he felt he was seventy years young. He also told me that his dog had died. Of course he did not speak: I learned these things through his silence.

I then told him of my dog, the one I had met in the Antarctic.

He then replied that he felt sorry for people who did not realize that dogs were not really dogs. His own, he said, had told him he would be reincarnated in Sikkim and that was why he was going there to find him. He said he and his dog were complementary. 'He will take the body of a dog so as to complete mine, and I will continue in this body of a youth of seventy in order to complete his. He does not see colours, and so I will help him with that. On the other hand, he sees God in scents and so far I can't do that. Anyhow, one thing we have in common is silence.'

I was deeply moved by what he said. 'Have you already reached the top of the Tree of Life?' I asked. 'Are you by any chance Padmasambhava? Perhaps that's why I didn't know you were Ernest when we first met.'

Now I see him far away in the mountains walking about and asking for his dog. He speaks to the tops of the trees and to the animals and birds that he meets. He is able to speak to them because he knows the language of silence.

'Have you seen my dog?' he asks, 'a very small dog with long blond hair, or perhaps his hair is dark.'

'What is his name?' they reply.

'I believe,' he answers, 'that it is Sulamite or Young Fawn, and *he must be grazing among the white lilies.*'

4 Return, return that we may look upon thee

Footsteps in the Sand

I have come back to the beaches of Madras. It is many years since the night I heard the fisherman playing his flute there, but there is much that is familiar. Walking barefoot across the sand, I gaze at the sea: it exhudes a heavy vapour, breathing like a strange prehistoric beast. In the distance the sun is setting, and the pale moon is rising. I look only at the sand, however, searching for lost footsteps. But of course I don't find them. Could it be that the surface of the world has changed over the years? Could it be that it changes once in each century?

Not far from the beach there are trees which used to have milky flowers growing in their branches. When I was here before, I climbed up to the high branches to pick the flowers. The thick liquid that oozed from their stems was like the moisture she remembered from the crushed grapes of the Valley of Ur. Now, however, the trees are bare: the branches are dry, and only the roots below the ground retain moisture.

With the coming of nightfall I lay down on the beach and listened to the deep rumble of the sea which in the white of the moon seemed to be speaking to me. I put my ear to the sand and listened. It's heart must be beating next to mine, I thought, for that is what happened when we sang the old songs here before. Then, as if in a trance, I reached out for her whom the years had engulfed long ago. In the blackness of the night I seemed to feel her fingers joined with mine, entwined by the flower of the Tree of Paradise.

Then I fell asleep beside the sea. Between dreams I thought I heard the voice of a child singing: *The mandrakes are loosening their perfumes*. And then I suddenly saw the blue god dancing over the sands to the rhythm of the flute. Blue and naked he came: he was both young and old, both man and woman. Golden horns sprouted from his head, and his flute was garlanded with feathers and flowers. He looked at me with a familiar smile and without stopping his song or his dance, he pointed to a place close by me. Then, as his golden fingernail rose and fell in the night, he exclaimed: 'Ecce OM!'

With that, he disappeared. But the moon remained, throwing a palpitating light on the sands. These sands are like the desert, I thought, and her feet must have walked here over the centuries, leaving their imprint.

Then, without knowing why, I began to dig at the spot indicated by the blue god who is also the heavenly shepherd. Deep below the surface I came upon a footprint. But there was blood there as well, and the foot had been badly bruised.

The Return of the Queen of Sheba

The Kulu Valley which is known as the Valley of the Gods is well within the Himalayas. It takes a long time to reach it, and the road goes through gentle hills covered with pine forests and fig trees. Flowers grow in the ravines but the apples are sour. High above the road on the snow-capped mountain peaks live the Gaddis. They are now nomad shepherds but once belonged to the warrior caste and are thought to have come from Rajasthan in India. They look like ancient Greeks: they have white skin, wear white caps and long robes which they knot round their waists with braided cords.

Crossing the Rotan Pass at an altitude of more than 13,000 feet, the road goes to Lahoul and Spiti, crosses the rain line and enters Tibet. There the light makes the mountains purple and there always seem to be barefoot pilgrims walking along the steep paths. Along the roadside are stones bearing the inscription, 'Om mane padme hum', which pilgrims and lamas have left behind them.

The last village before the Rotan Pass is called Manali. This town and the whole of the Kulu Valley is inhabited by a happy pagan people. Like the Gaddis, they came to this place after escaping from the Moghul invasion. They seem to be pure Aryans, although their rites and traditions are even older, coming perhaps from Dravidian times, from the Indus Valley or even, perhaps, from Atlantis. All through this Himalayan area the skin of the inhabitants is strangely suggestive. It is white like that of the Aryans, but is also spotted as though touched by the night that overwhelmed Atlantis or by the black complexion of the goddess Kali.

All the inhabitants of the Valley of the Gods have syphilis. It is an endemic disease which is transmuted from generation to generation, yet no one seems to be affected by it. The syphilitics of the Kulu Valley seem like true gods in their gaiety and beauty. There are no happier people. Syphilis has made them gods or perhaps, as gods, they are not affected by the disease.

They worship the ancient Rishis and each village has its own. These are Manu Rishi, Beas Rishi, Gautain Rishi, Vashist Rishi, Kastikswami Rishi and many others. When they are not working in their rice paddies or picking apples, the people beat drums and play the flute. They also sing and dance through the pine forests.

The women wear red kerchiefs and brightly coloured petticoats. Up on the mountainsides where they keep their herds of goats, they invite passers-by to make love. In this way they pass on their gay mountain spirit and their syphilis.

Their eyes are immensely bright but also deeply suggestive. As they bend over their rice paddies they sing to the wind:

O Mother,
Even Brahma and Indra who performed a hundred sacrifices,
Even all the Devas who live in heaven,
Who have all drunk the nectar which removes fear,
Even all these must one day die.
Only Siva,
Who drank the deadly poison,
Does not die,
Because of the greatness of his ear ornaments.

In the evening the whole valley resounds with the noise of cymbals and dancing. As the rhythm increases, the people come down from the hills and gather from distant villages. A procession forms which carries the god through the valley. His name is Manu Rishi and he dictated the code of law thousands of years ago. Now, however, he is reduced to a crude wooden doll. Like the inhabitants, he is probably syphilitic, and he is certainly impotent because he failed to bring rain. The procession has therefore been formed to punish him. He is being taken by the people to a temple in the woods where he will be shut up until it begins to rain.

Leading the procession is the Interpreter who wears a thick mountain dress and a braided straw cap. He dances a pantomime and acts as though he were having a difficult time pulling the litter bearing Manu Rishi to the temple. The stubborn god pretends to struggle and resist his punishment. As a result of this game, the Interpreter arrives at the temple quite exhausted from fighting with the wooden god.

At the temple the atmosphere is quite different. Here the people fall silent and only the Interpreter moves. Sweating and trembling, he drops to his knees and cries out:

O Chaste One,
Only Thy spouse lives at the time of the great dissolution.
All others die;
Brahma, Hari, Yama, Kubera,
All these die, and even the wakeful eyes of great Indra close.

The procession has arrived at the temple of Kali, who is the Mother, the wife, and the Devourer.

The wooden temple stands in the middle of some pine woods. It is typical of the Himalayas, for it has a curved pagoda roof and is extremely old. Round the entrance hang animal bones and the skulls of deer. In the courtyard of the temple there is an immense rock from which a flat projection rises like an altar. It is black and polished and human sacrifices have probably been made here. The rock antedates the temple, so that it is coloured as much by the waters of Atlantis as by the blood dedicated to Siva and to his black wife, Kali. In front of the altar there is a small wooden lingam, or phallus, which is adorned with flowers and with sour green apples.

In this enclosure, which is full of bats, the Manu Rishi is left. He appears to be crying in terror, and the villagers hope that his tears will be the rain that is needed in the rice fields.

In the meantime, outside of the temple, the Interpreter has fallen into a trance. People surround him and the drums beat faster and faster. Near by the sword dancers start their dance. Then suddenly everyone becomes silent, for by now the Interpreter is foaming at the mouth. His hair is wild and dishevelled and his body weaves back and forth. In this state, he is asked when the rains will come and he answers in the voice of Kali. 'The rain shall fall when the Black Wife is possessed by her Husband in the midst of her menstrual blood. Only then, only then will it rain!'

That night I suddenly woke up shivering and covered with perspiration. Outside my room I could hear a dog howling. I never thought I would hear that particular sound again. I was sure that my friend Sunya Bai had found his dog in Sikkim; therefore I presumed that this dog was the one I had known in the Antarctic. He had come to Manali in the Valley of the Gods, and had howled, as he had promised me he would do, when the Queen of Sheba returned. I had not expected, however, that he would howl with the same old fear and desperation. Therefore, I rose and with a trembling hand opened the door of my room. Outside the moon was full and I heard a drum sounding in the woods.

I looked about, but could not find the dog, nor did I see anybody. Then a shadow started to move at the end of the gravel pathway. It was the woman, Harijan, the wife of the untouchable whose family had cleaned latrines for more than two thousand years. Harijan means child of God. When the untouchable woman approached, I approached her and led her into my room. I turned on the light and saw her deep eyes and laughing mouth. She did not resist when I took off her clothes for she seemed to understand I was half fainting with fear, as one might tremble before the appearance of the whole continent of Atlantis. Her legs were long and thin but her feet were as rough as her hands, hardened with years of toil. Her breasts were small and soft, but her skin was stained and covered with dirt. She smelt of sheep and the rice fields.

Because of these things I had the impression I had laid that night with a dog. Besides, the woman was covered with menstrual blood.

Later on, when I again opened the door of my house and went out into the night air, I found it was raining. I could hear the drops falling in the rice paddies.

I ran down the stone path and the hillside. I was looking for my golden-haired dog. As I called out for him, I used the special whistle that I used as a child and which he also knows.

After a while I came to the Temple of Kali. I opened its small door and walked in. It was dark and I could hardly see. I imagined that I was being brushed by the wings of the bats that flew about inside, but now I think that what I felt was the moist tongue of my dog. After a little I was able to see the wooden doll, Manu Rishi, who was being punished, and so I spoke to him: 'You're free, Manu Rishi,' I said. 'It's raining outside, but only thanks to the woman you buried in the rice fields many thousands of years ago. The woman you enslaved has now given you liberty.'

But Manu Rishi didn't seem to be interested. He merely opened his wooden mouth. 'Don't talk so much,' he said; 'remember instead the brother of silence. Did you notice the earrings of the woman, Harijan? Thanks to her ornaments Siva was able to drink poison. That woman has never been a slave, and these people have never had syphilis. Do you know what that ear ornament really is? It is your friend Ernest. . . .'

By now I was trembling again from the cold rain that had seeped into my bones. I retired to a corner and sat down with my dog. Soon I began to feel very sleepy. In the meantime, the wooden doll was reciting:

O Father-Mother, I salute You!
You and your wife are one.
Begin the great dance!
The universe exists, yet it does not exist for you two.
And the eye of Indra opens. . . .

At the base of my vertebral column I began to feel very cold and stiff. I almost felt I was paralysed. Then, quite unexpectedly, my faithful dog licked me with his tongue. As he did so, I had a vision of the white fire of the oasis blazing forth, and I saw the Serpent of Paradise leaping towards the altar of Kali to seize the sour apple and so redeem the first temptation of the first husband and wife, Adam and Eve. It went up the tree, jumping from branch to branch and flower to flower. And in my forehead a moonstone appeared which was the eye of Indra slowly opening.

Then, with my breast almost bursting in that dark temple in the Valley of the Gods, I began to hear footsteps draw near. As the noise grew louder, the lingam of Siva began to swell towards the black stone altar of Kali which in turn began to look like the woman, Harijan, whom I had possessed in my bed in the hills. At last, through the milky crystal of my moonstone, I perceived the Queen of Sheba standing on the black altar and carrying her silver Kundalini. She called to me and ordered me to approach so that I might die next to the altar. My dog and I approached, and as we made ready for death we sang together these words:

Glory! To you of the three eyes,
To you who are frenzied
To you who are old
To you who are young.
Praise! To you who are Father
To you who are Mother and Female and Dog,
To you who are all things
And to you who are beyond all things.
Honour! To you, O murdering Mother!

As everything was slowly swallowed by the shadows that surrounded that primeval rock, a naked creature was being created again, with two earrings, one a man's, the other a woman's, and having the shape of a star as well as the sacred syllable OM.

This was the return and the marriage of the Queen of Sheba.

5 Ever since the Queen of Sheba went away I have been sitting alone

The Guest

The illusory figure created on the black altar is Ardhanarisvara. He wears the androgynous earrings which celebrate the sacred syllable OM, also written as AUM. The significance of this syllable is that A stands for Brahma who represents the dawn, U stands for Vishnu the guardian of noon-time, while M signifies Siva who presides over the night.

Ardhanarisvara was formed on the sacrificial altar by mixing the blood of the woman, Harijan, with my blood and the blood of my dog. This illusory being was made by the delicate hands of the Queen of Sheba. They were touched by the madness of God and were scratched by the sands of the desert. She was sacrificed to create the illusion of Ardhanarisvara, and as her blood mixed with ours, she also died.

The marriage has come about. But for a proper marriage feast, a wedding guest must be present. He, finally, creates the whole illusion and presides over the sacrifice of so many beings. For this reason, there was a guest at this wedding, a figure who stepped towards the altar and leaned on a cross around which was entwined a serpent with the head of a dragon. Joining the palms of his hands, he began to pray, speaking the following words:

Earth covers the feet up to the knees: there kneel the rice roots.
Water reaches from the knees to the abdomen: there the dog licks the soles of the woman, Harijan.
Fire rises from the stomach to the throat: there the Queen of Sheba lives and dreams.
Air envelopes the throat and forehead: there the moonstone grows.
What is invisible is where I am.

The guest then fell on his knees and wept:

I have joined my hands.
The thumb is fire, the forefinger air, the middle finger earth, the fourth finger water and the little finger the sky.
When I have joined all these I have created you, O Ardhanarisvara, because I have sacrificed myself.
You and I become one. The Father and the son are one person.

After the marriage comes the marriage feast. At the marriage of the Queen of Sheba, the wedding guest, standing beside the altar of Atlantis, was devoured by the serpent that clung to his cross. This had to be because the name of the wedding guest was Jesus Christ.

The Servants

One day while at a party conversing about all these things, I noticed that somebody had left a cigarette case behind. I picked it up and saw that it had many compartments, one of which was for cigarette holders. It looked quite old and was almost falling apart. One of the holders in the case was for smoking opium and was decorated with an almost illegible inscription. For a long while I wondered whether or not I should use it; I hesitated because it seemed to me that cigarette holders are too private and personal to be used by other people.

I walked up and down thinking about the matter and after a while a friend came up to me. Without my having to explain anything, he said to me: 'As usual, you are trying to profit from somebody else's work. You are really very stupid.'

Immediately I understood what he meant, and so I answered: 'I see that you are Melchizedek. You're right: I am stupid. On the other hand, you are not. For myself, I have never known how to do the intermediate steps, and I'm even ignorant of what is essential. There's no use in my studying because I never remember anything. Therefore I must turn to you because you know. Thanks to your wisdom the Queen of Sheba came back. But when you die I'm going to have you thrown into your pot of chemicals. I am quite willing to admit that I'm afraid the Queen of Sheba may discover how much you know and how little I know.'

While I was speaking, the orchestra began to play some old music, and so when I was finished I asked my friend not to go away but to sit with me and listen to it. I told him there was a secret rhythm that lay behind the notes we heard, and I explained that it was the rhythm of drums played by negroes. I told him that if he stayed with me, we would create something remarkable between us. He of course was an alchemist, but I felt within me all that was necessary for the creation of our artificial being. In addition, I could sense the presence of all the 'works and days of hands'. At one end were the red hands, next came the yellow and the white, and over all were the black hands for they were the ones that played the drums.

A dead woman then came up to us and began to prophesy and warn us, but when we looked at her hands we saw they were lined. Then we knew she was an impostor, for death removes the lines from all hands.

The truth is that I came to understand a good deal at this party. I knew who the servants were, and knew that as we use them so they use us and indeed alter us, as do the black children along the beaches of Madras. I realized that one cannot be everything at once. One is either a scientist or a man who understands the essence. One is either Melchizedek or Solomon.

As I left I thanked all the servants, nodding my head to all of them, men and women, children and animals, to all who since my childhood have been modelling and sustaining me with their multicoloured hands, preparing me for matrimony and death.

Melchizedek

Melchizedek was the chief priest of Solomon's kingdom. He was also a magician and an alchemist and was much beloved of Solomon. For many years they worked and talked together, and there were no auguries to disturb them. Then one day Melchizedek looked up at the sky across the desert and, turning to Solomon, he said: *Who is this that cometh out of the wilderness like a pillar of smoke, perfumed with myrrh and frankincense?* He pointed towards a distant caravan moving across the desert. Thus it was that Melchizedek was the first to see the Queen of Sheba and to speak the phrase that is repeated in the Song of Songs.

Solomon paid no attention to Melchizedek because he was at that time busy imparting justice, and had arranged the sword to be suspended over the child. And so Melchizedek put on his sandals and dressed in his best robe. He spent a whole night walking across the desert, and when dawn came, he reached the outposts of the royal caravan. There he asked for the name of the visitor and was told that it was a woman who had come to the Kingdom of Solomon in search of the wise man, Melchizedek, who she had heard was a magician and alchemist who knew the great mysteries.

Thus it is curious but true that the Queen of Sheba did not go to Solomon's kingdom to look for Solomon but to see Melchizedek. It must also have been fate that drew Melchizedek's steps to her caravan so that he would be the first in the kingdom to meet her. They met on a small hill at a few moments after dawn in the desert sands, halfway between Ur and Solomon.

The Queen came on a blue camel, and round her arm a snake was twisted. She looked down upon Melchizedek and spoke to him: 'Why did you come ahead of time? I did not expect to find you here but rather next to your famous cauldron where you mix the elements.'

When he looked into her deep eyes, Melchizedek recognized there shadows of the lost continent of Atlantis and he knew that she had partaken of the ancient drama that had taken place in Paradise. He knew that her snake was the serpent from the Garden of Eden.

'I have been waiting for you,' he answered. '*Come to my chamber, and I will give you the most exquisite wine.* We shall see what to do with the snake and I will make you ready for the chamber of Solomon.'

When Melchizedek uttered this last mechanical statement of loyalty to his king, the Queen of Sheba lowered her head, and Melchizedek noticed that her forehead was as high as the disc of the moon.

For a long time the Queen of Sheba remained in Melchizedek's house, studying and preparing herself. Solomon was unaware of her presence for he was always busy with justice and the division of the child by the sword.

Melchizedek remained seated next to his cauldron, putting in amaranth drops and mixing in emeralds, mercury, blue sapphires and peacock's feathers.

'From these substances,' he said, 'the Bird of Paradise will be created, and we shall watch its birth together. It's a rare bird last seen at Avalon on the continent of Atlantis.'

An odour of myrrh, sandalwood and jasmin rose from the cauldron. The Queen of Sheba watched Melchizedek with fascination, for she had always liked perfumes, and it is said that she invented them.

'Do you suppose,' she asked, 'that you could produce a scent that would bring about immortality?'

'Only if you were to throw your snake into the cauldron and only if you threw yourself in afterwards. If you did that I would follow you. But first we need the Bird of Paradise.'

With these words, the bird was created, and there on the floor of Melchizedek's house in the city of Solomon, the Bird of Paradise began to dance. It moved from side to side, dangling its head as though it were searching for something. Then it moved back and forth between Melchizedek and the Queen of Sheba. For days and weeks, from dawn

6 Even all the Devas who live in heaven, all these must one day die

until evening, it continued its dance. It was completely alone and oblivious of its creators. Then one day it jumped onto the lid of the cauldron where it continued its dance. But now its dance was stationary and only the feathers moved, rapidly opening and closing. Then suddenly the incredible happened. In its madness the bird became like a god. The feathers began to grow and soon all of Melchizedek's house was filled with them. And the diamonds and emeralds of these feathers were like the eyes of the Queen of Sheba which began to take on a new understanding.

It would almost seem, too, that Solomon had also begun to feel this strange force, for he interrupted his work of imparting justice. The sword remained on high, and he returned the child whole to the true mother. He had imparted justice without knowing it.

Then the bird disappeared: it never really existed since it was a Bird of Paradise.

Melchizedek put his head between his hands and began to speak: 'Thus far and thus far only can we go. It is too dangerous to go farther. Yet it is also dangerous not to go on, for only once in eternity is this miracle possible. Everything becomes symbolic, but unfortunately we haven't enough symbols. Gestures have different meanings although they are the same gestures. They become the images of love, yet they are not love. But here we must take a chance. A moment ago you mentioned a perfume; are you ready to begin?'

'What must I do?' asked the Queen of Sheba.

'You must take off your clothes and come into the cauldron with me. The snake will go in between your legs and will come out between your eyes. The perfume will then be for both of us.'

She looked at him without moving: 'I have come on a pilgrimage,' she said, 'but I don't know whether we can do this without love.'

Melchizedek raised his head and in his eyes there was a look of deep suffering.

'If we stop here,' he said, 'then only disaster can come. Atlantis will sink once again beneath the waves. Only once in a million years do we have this opportunity. You should know that because you have spent years searching, years wandering in torment over the sands. The cauldron is now ready and the feathers of the Bird of Paradise are waiting for the snake. . . .'

But the Queen of Sheba hesitated. She stood next to the cauldron but did not move because she had no love for Melchizedek. She had admired the fantastic dance of the bird but was also repelled by it. She knew that if she entered the cauldron, her torments would be over, but she was not altogether sure that she wanted them to end. For all her centuries of wandering she still felt youth leaping like a fawn in her heart. Yet she knew that she had come across the sands from Ur for a particular purpose, and now Melchizedek was waiting for her to do her part.

Still she waited at the edge of the cauldron. She hesitated and let her arms hang down so that one by one her veils fell from her, revealing her perfumed hair and the forehead that looks like the disc of the moon. She inclined a little towards the snake, her lips were half-opened and her eyes were staring. She stood naked with her small breasts like two young roes and with her long legs slightly apart.

Melchizedek rose up and let his robe fall from his shoulders. He took a rod—perhaps it was Aaron's—and went to touch her. She then transformed her snake into another rod, but neither sprouted a flower.

'We must first embrace each other,' Melchizedek began, but before he could finish the sentence, a cloud of vapour arose from the cauldron and enveloped the Queen of Sheba, making her invisible. Then the Bird of Paradise who had not died but who was waiting on the floor of Melchizedek's house, rose up and flew out of the window towards Solomon's temple. This bird spread the news of the Queen of Sheba's arrival, betraying Melchizedek. It entered Solomon's chamber, bearing with it the perfumes of Atlantis, and told the king that Melchizedek had prepared the Queen of Sheba for himself.

Solomon hung up the sword of justice, put on his sandals and his best robe and looked out at the rising sun. He felt the bird singing in his heart and sensed the paradise it signified. But he also remembered the snake.

Before going to Melchizedek's house, Solomon wanted to be convinced that his action was just, so he went to see the most ancient wise man of his city, a man who in former years had been Melchizedek's teacher. He found the master seated beside his sphinx. He was talking to himself: 'Right here the other world sank beneath the waves. Now the signal has been heard which announces the birth of a new world. Yet no one understands it: only those who are mad can comprehend, and only those who know how to love.'

'Master,' began Solomon, 'I have come to ask whether any world can be submerged without love, or whether any body can be submerged, be it the body of a queen or of a slave.'

'You speak well,' answered the master, 'for a king is always a slave.'

'Yes, I am a slave of justice,' replied Solomon.

'Forget justice and be a king,' was the answer. 'To love is to forget justice. To love is to lose oneself: to drown oneself in the boiling cauldron of Melchizedek, to risk a kingdom and drown on Atlantis. I taught Melchizedek, and I also built the Sphinx.'

'Did you do it without love, Master?'

'I will answer you like the Sphinx. I did it beyond justice: I did it with the number three. Three is beyond two, and in two there is no repose or rest. I did it with three because three is beyond repose or rest: it is beyond happiness or sadness and has no limits. It is like a mist that rises and encircles and then disappears. It comes and it goes, but even when it goes it is still there in spirit. Yet while it is beyond justice, it is close to crime and murder. In dividing the child with a sword, you satisfy the false mother, who is really the true one. When you think you have been just you have not been just. When you are unjust you are with God because you are loving. . . .'

'But Master,' replied Solomon, 'I want to go down in history as a just king.'

'You must love . . . . You must kill Melchizedek!'

'That is suicide. Melchizedek is my brother; if I kill him I kill myself.'

'You must have the courage to die. It's all one. Look at the Sphinx: it is a fish, an animal, a bird, a man. I am you and you are the Queen of Sheba. Love yourself and love the Queen of Sheba as yourself. From the depths of the seas you will return as a fish or a bird or a slave, or as a king or a queen. Melchizedek is already dead, and from his ashes will rise the Song of Songs. It belongs to him, but history will attribute it to you.'

Solomon rose and left the wise man and walked slowly towards the house of Melchizedek. His head hung low and in his hand he carried a staff which looked like a serpent.

He entered the house without knocking. He knew the house well, for he had often gone there to watch Melchizedek mix his elements. He had passed hours there observing his friend's alchemy.

When Solomon opened the door of the secret alcove, he found Melchizedek leaning over his cauldron, trying to discover the strange substance that had created the cloud that made the Queen of Sheba invisible. It was easy for Solomon to push him into the cauldron, and Melchizedek sank instantly. His death was like a preordained symbol. He himself had hoped for it as the only possibility for eternity. In a sense he had always been at the bottom of the cauldron. When he fell, his last sigh was one of love for Solomon, and thus his death opened the way to number three. From the depths of the cauldron rose the Song of Songs.

Immediately the mists that had enveloped the Queen of Sheba parted, and she presented her first gift to the king. It was a golden mantle from the city of Ur. He in turn gave her his carved staff which looked like a serpent. It was the rod of Aaron, and from its end a flower bloomed. It was a jasmin from Atlantis.

She played this staff like a flute and together they sang the Song of Songs.

On his knees, kissing her long legs, the king then spoke: 'I am not a wise man like Melchizedek. I know nothing: I don't know how to mix the elements. All I can do is sing the Song of Songs, and I am sorry that it isn't even my song.'

'That doesn't matter,' she replied. 'Only the blue bird which I sent to your window is for you.'

'But the Song of Songs isn't mine!'

'It is yours. *Thou, my king, take me to your secret chamber and let me drink there your most exquisite wine*. Melchizedek said that, but remember that you and he were one.'

'Do you believe, my Queen, that Melchizedek could be Solomon? Do you really believe that he was the same as me? If that was so, then the story of Solomon and the Queen of Sheba would have been very different. Think what would have happened if the Queen of Sheba had obeyed the mysterious incantations of Melchizedek and had thrown herself into the cauldron with him without love! That would have broken the cross of creation, and stopped the flow of history. It would have prevented reincarnation and given you peace in your tomb. But what a tragedy to have killed my wise brother, to have destroyed Melchizedek and lost the only opportunity to come in a million years. Melchizedek and I are not the same yet only I know how to sing the Song of Songs even though it really belongs to him. There's only one more thing for us to do: we must go together into the boiling cauldron and drown ourselves with Melchizedek. That will give birth to the number three, will give intelligence to love and allow it to be united with wisdom. *Come, my beloved, my dove, my spouse, come. . . .*'

From the boiling cauldron which drowned them, like the flood that submerged Atlantis, rose a gentle hymn, the bleating of a lamb.

For the Song of Songs is the bravery of the lamb sacrificed in the burning bush.

7 However fast or slow the Queen of Sheba runs we will never catch up with her

The Lamb

When I was in the ice fields of the Antarctic, I had a sheep dog rather than a husky. Since he was unaccustomed to the ices, he died there, but while he lived he looked after the sheep and protected them from thieves. When he died there was no one left to look after the lamb. A lamb can only survive when it is protected by a dog.

It may seem paradoxical, but no one can kill a dog without killing a lamb along with it. Perhaps they have a kinship through their warm white fleece.

On the other hand no one ever sacrifices a dog: a lamb is considered sufficient. The relationship between these two animals suggests that a lamb is a dog who has learned to bleat, having mastered the Song of Songs. This process is not so unnatural when you consider the delicate rose that grows from the bramble bush.

The dog lies at the root of our childhood, resting at the base of the cross where instincts sleep, while the lamb grows up by the crossbar and eventually rises to the heights where he will find eternal love and life, the rose and the Queen of Sheba.

If life were not like that, it would end in disaster. After all, the Great Mother always consumes the dog and devours the man with her love. She is irresistible. All you can do is change the victim, and replace the dog or the man by the lamb. In this way, the dog and the man are saved, although there is still doubt concerning the salvation of God.

The lamb hangs from the cross with his fleece dishevelled and his flesh torn and consumed. It has been like this throughout history and so it will be for eternity. But the lamb never quite dies; he is always saved by his golden fleece.

The Lamb

The small boy was saved from the burning bush and was neither eaten nor sacrificed. Instead a lamb was substituted. Meanwhile, the child's dog, who had always been his companion in the fields, survives and grows old with him.

Lamb's flesh will always be food for the gods since it satisfies the Mother's hunger. This is flesh created in Melchizedek's cauldron with knowledge gained from Atlantis, cradled by the Queen of Sheba and praised by Solomon in the Song of Songs.

The lamb is the son of man. It is a flower that grows in the ice floes; it is the fiery rose of the Cross.

The Bird of Paradise

This bird has so far been neglected, but it is very important, since through it one can perhaps go beyond the Great Mother and escape her influence. Born among flames, nurtured by the Song of Songs, it can fly as easily to the heights as to the depths. It is even possible that it existed long before man.

Its dance is the most serious effort attempted since the creation, since more than anything else it gives form to life.

At dawn the forest is heavy with shadows, but with the first rays of the sun, the Bird of Paradise awakens from his perch on the branch of a tree. He stretches his neck and pecks at the wood with his beak. He is still sleepy and cannot see properly. Then he begins to be more alert and to look from side to side. He seems to be afraid of something —perhaps of an attack. He moves his head about and looks at the sun, as though he were asking for an invitation to life itself. His action is completely unconscious; it is something inbred in his deepest instincts. He wants action, he wants to take part, yet at the same time he is afraid. He has longed for what is about to happen, but he would also like to avoid it. *Father, if it be possible, let this cup pass from me.*

From his childhood the Bird of Paradise always had more to do with his father than with his mother. Several other birds and animals have similar relationships. The dog I had in the Antarctic was like that.

When the sun rises a little higher, and the green forest becomes tinged with gold, the bird flies down from his branch to the earth. There the mists of the night are being drawn up by the sun's rays, and the bird begins to move in circles. Then he traces squares within the circles he has drawn. Somehow he seems to be caught there; he stops to look at what he has done, and he seems intelligent. At the same time he is nervous and afraid. He wonders why he stays where he is, and he wonders whether he has asked for something that is no longer possible. He suspects he is engaged in a farce, as though he were consciously trying to deceive himself, or occupy himself with details that have long since lost their importance—such as why feathers come loose or leaves fall from the trees. Yet at the same time, one feels that a force has begun to dominate this bird, that he will soon be in convulsions. His eyes are now open in terror and he is thinking about his father.

Just then there is a flapping of wings and two female birds come into the forest clearing. First they watch with curiosity, but soon they are astonished by the dance of the Bird of Paradise. They are both females of the species, and only yesterday they met him. Yesterday they flew together, ate together, loved and slept together. Yesterday the Bird of Paradise showed them the steps of another dance. But today they do not understand what he is doing. Now he is alone; he has forgotten them utterly and they, recognizing his voice, realize that although it is the same it is not directed towards them. First they are a little hurt and saddened, as mothers are, but soon they become resigned and watch him with pious expressions.

The Bird of Paradise is wholly unaware of the birds. He is in a trance, hermetically sealed in a dream. On and on he dances. He dances under the noon sun, and towards the evening he is still dancing. By sundown he has danced so much that a wound has opened in his side. The female birds staunch the flow of his blood with their beaks.

This is an ancient drama and will continue to be repeated through the centuries. The mothers realize they must do something or else they will be separated by the father's triumph.

Once again night comes to the forest: the owls come forth and stars shine in the sky. On the next day the Bird of Paradise begins his dance again. The female birds come again and watch, fascinated by what they so dislike.

During the next night, the Bird of Paradise asks for water, but no one gives him any. By now there are two festering sores on his hands.

For days the dance continues: the bird is in a complete trance, oblivious of everything about him. His eyes are closed to what happens outside: they only look inside, as if in search for the secret there. But what is about to happen will be seen by no one, because by now even the female birds have left. It's possible they have entered the wound in his side, and that the wound is only reopened, since the female birds were first created out of his side. But what is more likely is that they have gone down to the bottom of the forest to wait. Mother love has the patience of centuries behind it. The females believe that the Bird of Paradise has gone mad and that he will soon die. They are merely waiting until the time comes when they must return to the clearing of the forest, to stroke his dead feathers and to eat his flesh. Love is hunger: it is a desire to fuse essences. It is literally a holy communion.

Once more the Bird of Paradise flies up to the highest branch. There he leans back and turns his face to the sun. At this point the incredible miracle occurs. Out of his small crumpled form of feathers comes a huge mountain of plumes. They are golden feathers, light blue lace, pearls, emeralds, rubies and diamonds. It is the crown of Siva, the dancing god; it is a crown of thorns made of suns and stars and planets. The bird in his triumph resists the force within him, yet at the same time revels in his ecstasy. Then, pierced through by its mystery, the diminutive yet enormous Bird of Paradise begins to sing, *My father and I are one*. And another white bird descends from the heavens to kiss him.

The Mass

From all directions the faithful pilgrims move towards Mount Kailas. They have already washed in the sacred waters of Lake Manasarovar; they have been baptized by John and have been transformed. Free from sin, they are now ready to sin again.

Up above, on the summit of the mountain, dances the Lord Siva. After penetrating the wound of his divine wife, Parvati, he has entered her and become part of her in an eternal embrace. It is for this reason that Siva dances happily in the light and in the shade.

On the other side of the mountain is the lamasery of Dirapukh. It is night, and a young lama is about to celebrate a rite for which he has been preparing for fourteen years. It is the first time the rite will take place and also the last. Seated on the cold ground he beats a drum with the bones of dead men. Again and again he strikes the drum until at length all is prepared. The lama then undresses and steps naked into the cold night air. He invokes the Lord Buddha because he does not worship Siva at least by that name, and he says, 'Om mane padme hum.' He then turns towards the four quarters, beginning to walk from left to right, which is the reverse of the direction used for climbing. Ready now to sacrifice himself to the visible and invisible presences, the young lama calls out: *Here is my body—Eat it!* But in fact the young lama is afraid someone might come. There are twelve invisible figures who are his masters and who have taught him this rite and who now silently wait with him. When nothing happens the young lama calls out again: 'Here I am, ready to be consumed.'

At this, the twelve masters throw themselves on the young man and begin to devour him. As he feels his skin being torn, the young lama is terrified, but he does not cry out despite his terrible pain. Soon he has lost a leg, then his arms and his face, and a moment later his entrails. During the whole ghastly sacrifice the young man has been in an agony, but once it is concluded, he becomes calm and happy. He has grown larger in the sacrifice for he is now in twelve bodies. And the young lama, now without bones, blood or body of any kind, knows that he is up above, dancing on the summit of Mount Kailas, beyond the barriers of shadow and sunlight.

On another mountain someone is slowly climbing. He too has had his body washed by John, though as he drowned it in the water, he emerged with the head of a lamb. Now he carries a cross, and slowly from right to left he climbs the hill. He is going to pay for a great sin because he was unable to make it rain. Now he is at the summit with the two thieves. Earlier they had tried, darkly, to discover what misery really was and to pass over it in order to dance in the light and in the shadow. As simple men they had resisted facing the sordid misery of mankind. They constituted the number two. Now, however, with the arrival of another, they are three together and they feel rested. No longer are they alone. And at the end, even though they do not hear what he says, they are going to die in peace, the good as well as the evil, as much one as another.

One, two and three. . . . But where is the fourth?

There, below the cross, is the fourth. One, two, three and four. Two thieves, a redeemer and the mother. Two thieves, a redeemer and the earth. In reality they are all one person, because the Father is not part of this. He is to be found before the beginning of numbers, and Christ and the Mother are the same person. When I opened the coffin of the Mother, I found that she had the body of the Queen of Sheba as well as that of Jesus Christ.

Afterwards, when the Father appeared to have abandoned him, and when he groaned and died, the Mother gave the signal for the cross to be lowered. They did not lower him, however, without pulling up the cross as well. Then the twelve disciples carried it down to the tomb, which in reality is the altar, and there they ate him while he was still

8 If I had a white horse I would be able to catch up with the Queen of Sheba

nailed to the cross. The Mother did not touch him, however, because she had already devoured him before.

When the women came afterwards they were unable to find him, for he had already been eaten. They knew this, but told it to no one.

When I open the coffin of my soul I know that I am celebrating a mass, that I am devouring myself and becoming one with the body of the redeemer. The sacrificer and the sacrificed are always one and the same, and in the sacred rite of the mass, the priest murders Christ and eats him. The first priest was Melchizedek who came from Salem, and Melchizedek was the lamb of Abraham and the deer of Rama. It was he who taught me how to mix the wine and the water and to drink it from the hollow of the hands of the Queen of Sheba. He also taught me how to consecrate my own blood by drinking it and to redeem my own flesh by eating it.

I have now pulled out all the nails and have opened the tomb, and inside I have found only bones. Once again I have therefore closed it up, but the air has stirred all the ancient memories.

My trinity, too, is different from others. In mine, the son is a daughter, and the father is the daughter's husband. I who am her brother walk at her side. I love her surreptitiously and have married her secretly so that he will never separate us. We come along, all three of us together, with our hands joined, at once happy and suffering, walking towards a place that is so far away I can see nothing of it at all.

The White Horse

If I had a white horse I would be able to catch up with the Queen of Sheba. The fast horse I need has a rider on his back, called Kalki, who carries a sword and who comes to judge.

The mystery I have spoken of will remain for future generations to solve. I myself am beginning to understand it a little but that is only because of the misery I have suffered since the Queen of Sheba left me. Man in misfortune is always searching. What I am looking for is something more speedy than the Queen of Sheba, a white steed that will allow me to catch up with her.

I will try to put this in another way.

Consider time. Everybody knows what time is. It is something which burns, it is something which is spent. Then there is light. Among other things, light is wastage of form. Since it escapes, it is like the Queen of Sheba. Light brings us images and little by little reveals legends. Light is the future, and the end of the future is the last image. It is also the end of time. However fast or slow the Queen of Sheba runs we will never catch up with her. The light which carries our images towards the cosmos steals our infancy, our youth and our entire life. Between the two thieves, time has us crucified. They are quicker than we are. Time pierces us with a ray of light and thus exhausts and wastes us. Overcome by these forces, our only hope is Kalki, the rider of the white horse, whose energy is even greater than those of light and time.

If we were able to climb up to a star and to move faster than light then we would catch up with the Queen of Sheba, and we would regain our lost infancy and arrive at a time before we were born. The white horse and Kalki always ride in a direction contrary to time; they run towards the past. Thus instead of growing old, we would grow younger and become eternal.

Once the Queen of Sheba was caught on the ray of a star, she would go no farther but would join the horse and the rider, and the marriage would be complete.

Another way of describing this is to call it the last judgment and the resurrection of the flesh. The light will be judged for having stolen the images and the flesh will be revived: bodies will again come to life if their images are overtaken by the white horse which gallops towards the past. Everything will once again exist in a quiet central point where time at last is calm and still.

There are those who think that this miracle will be given us by science, but I think it is more likely to be given us by Christ, because after all, he is the rider of the white horse.

He is the one force among us that is stronger than light. To explain it in ancient words, it is he who judged the thieves and pardoned them, who overcame time and caught up with the Queen of Sheba. In truth he married her and pulled her up to join him on the white horse.

But so that all this may take place, I too have had to marry the Queen of Sheba, so that I might prepare both my weddings and my death.

It is extremely difficult to explain all this, even with ancient words.

The Last Flower

Even though you are *married*, you will have to die one day. Everybody has to die. The difference for the person who is *married* is this: that a youth will come carrying a flower which he will touch to your lips and to your forehead. Possibly the flower will come alone. If it does, then you will leap directly into that flower and remain there. It seems a difficult feat, but it is the result of hard work and of the waiting you have endured during your life, especially the waiting for your wedding. But it really makes no difference whether the youth comes: because the flower you enter is the final fruit of your soul and your ultimate creation.